For the little cat Miro . . .
—A.D.

To Liam and Thierry for their love.
—L.C.

Books published by Running Press are available at special discounts for bulk purchases in the United States
by corporations, institutions, and other organizations.
For more information, please contact the Special Markets Department at the Perseus Books Group,
2300 Chestnut Street, Suite 200, Philadelphia, PA 19103, or call (800) 810-4145, ext. 5000,
or e-mail special.markets@perseusbooks.com.

ISBN 978-0-7624-5409-9
Library of Congress Control Number: 2014931177

9 8 7 6 5 4 3 2 1
Digit on the right indicates the number of this printing

Designed by T.L. Bonaddio
Edited by Marlo Scrimizzi
Typography: Archer, Pompiere, and The Only Exception

Published by Running Press Kids
An Imprint of Running Press Book Publishers
A Member of the Perseus Books Group
2300 Chestnut Street
Philadelphia, PA 19103–4371

Visit us on the web!
www.runningpress.com/kids

Oh My, Oh No!

Lisa Charrier

translated by William Rodarmor

illustrated by
Agnès Domergue

RP|KIDS
PHILADELPHIA • LONDON

One day, I see Mommy drinking from a cup.
I go to drink out of it, too, but she says,

Oh my, oh no!

You mustn't drink that, sweetie!
It isn't good! It's coffee!
It's yucky!

But if it isn't good, why is she drinking it?
Mommy doesn't make any sense.

I want to be a big girl, just like Mommy.
So when I go to the bathroom, I wipe myself.

Oh my, oh no!

Why did you put toilet paper everywhere?

I'm being neat, Mommy.
I want everything nice and clean.

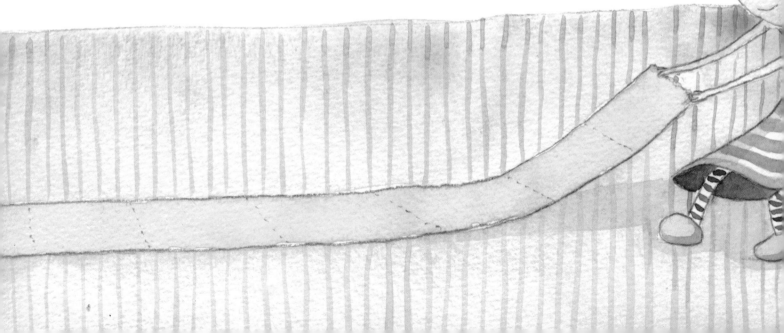

Mommy gives me some pretty paintbrushes.
To make her happy,
I paint pictures everywhere.

Oh my, oh no!

Why are you painting all over everything?

Mommy doesn't like art very much.

Mommy's mopping the floor. Everything sparkles.
I mop, too, just like Mommy.

Oh my, oh no!

What are you doing?
There's water everywhere!

Can't she see?
I want to help her.
Sometimes Mommy doesn't understand anything.

With a big smile, Mommy gives me a piece of cake.
With a big smile, I give my cake to the cat.
Mommy says,

Oh my, oh no!

Why'd you do that?
The cake is for you, not for Kitty-cat!

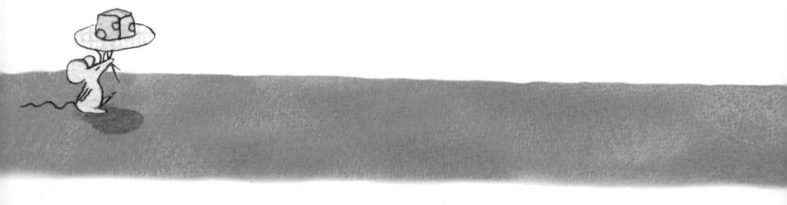

Doesn't Mommy know Kitty-cat's hungry?

Mommy shows me how to bake a cake.
I love cooking with her.
And I'm gonna make her a big surprise!

Oh my, oh no!

What have you done with the flour, darling?
It's all over the kitchen!

"Happy birthday, Mommy!
I made you a big white cake!"

When Mommy comes out of the bathroom,
she looks beautiful. I go into the bathroom to surprise her.

Oh my, oh no!

You've got makeup all over your face!
My jewelry's everywhere!
And look at my dress!

My surprise sure was a big success!

Mommy likes books.
She reads to me every night.
I'm reading a book to Mommy, and she laughs.

Oh my, oh no!

That's not the right way.
You're holding it upside down!

Mommy can't even recognize a picture upside down!

Mommies are strange.
They can't understand everything.

She's too tall.

up to here!

She goes from here . . .

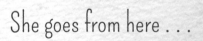

So Mommy can't see things the way I can.

Because I go from here . . .

to here!

She has a head, just like I do,

but it's full of all sorts of complicated questions.

She talks too fast and uses lots of words,

so she doesn't have any time to think!

But when I go to hug her,
we smile at each other with our eyes.
She understands me.

And that's the most important thing of all.

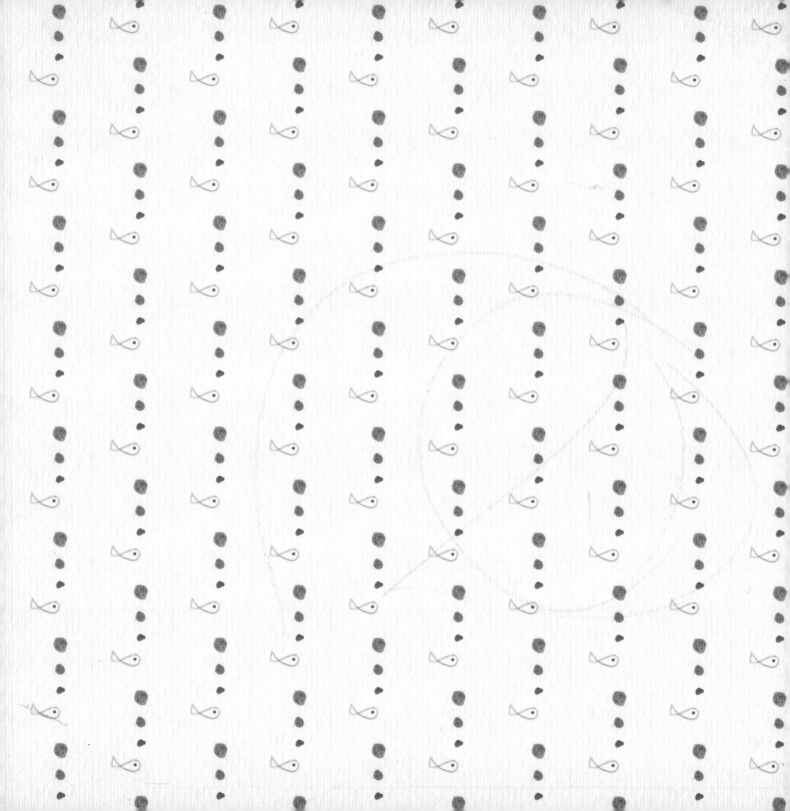